STONE WARRIORS RULE!

by Paul Mantell and Avery Hart

D0980727

A PARACHUTE PRESS BOOK

SCHOLASTIC INC.

New York Toronto London Auckland Sydney

A PARACHUTE PRESS BOOK
Parachute Press, Inc.
156 Fifth Avenue
New York, NY 10010

With special thanks to Hunter Heller, Lisa Ramee,
and Robyn Tynan-Winters.

Printed in the U.S.A.
November 1995
ISBN: 0-590-59876-7
A B C D E F G H I J

PROLOGUE

Castle Wyvern, Scotland: A.D. 994

We Gargoyles are an ancient race. Humans have always feared us. It is the nature of humans to fear what they cannot understand. Their ways are not our ways.

We are stone by day. But as the sun sets we become flesh and blood. We come alive! Then we have great

1

strength—greater than the strength of any human. But at night we bleed like humans do. And like humans, we can die.

I am called Goliath. I am the leader of the Gargoyles. For many years I and my fellow Gargoyles guarded Castle Wyvern and all who lived there. We guarded Princess Katharine and her people; the captain of the castle guards and his soldiers; and the Magus, the princess's powerful magician. We protected them all.

But the humans were not grateful. The princess insulted us. She called us monsters.

One female Gargoyle, who was my second-in-command, grew bitter and angry because of this. "We are better than humans," she swore. "We have lived here longer. One day we Gargoyles will rule!"

There was one human who agreed

with her—our friend, the captain. He thanked us for protecting the castle from its enemies. "Without your help, who knows what might happen? All in Castle Wyvern might be destroyed," he said.

The captain liked Gargoyles better than humans. So he made a deal with the enemy, the Vikings. The captain would let them attack the castle, as long as they left the Gargoyles alone. That night, the night when the Vikings were going to attack, the captain ordered the Gargoyles to leave the castle. But I did not know of his bargain. I, Goliath, ordered my second-in-command to stay behind with the other Gargoyles. "Protect the castle," I told her. "It is all we have."

I went in search of the Vikings, taking one friend with me—the wise old Gargoyle who had been the leader before me. But the Vikings had tricked us. While we were gone, the Vikings came. They attacked the castle at sunrise, when the Gargoyles were turned back to stone and could not fight.

When the old one and I returned to the castle, most of the Gargoyles were smashed to bits! Only three Gargoyle youngsters and our faithful watchdog remained. The others—gone! All gone! My second-in-command was gone, too—gone forever!

The castle was in ruins. The Gargoyles were blamed. The castle magician—the Magus—cast a spell over my companions, turning them to stone by day *and* night. The Gargoyles would sleep as stone—perched on top of Castle Wyvern until the castle should rise above the clouds.

"Cast your spell on me, too," I begged the Magus. "Turn me to stone like the others! I do not wish to live alone!"

So now the Magus is ready to cast his spell.

Farewell. Perhaps my friends and I shall never wake again. For castles cannot rise above the clouds…or can they?

CHAPTER 1

New York City: One Thousand Years Later...

David Xanatos stood on the roof of the Eyrie Building. It was his skyscraper—the tallest in New York City. And now it was taller than before, for there was a castle perched on top of it. A castle with stone Gargoyles!

Xanatos had bought the castle in

Wyvern, Scotland. Then he had brought it to New York, stone by stone. Xanatos was young, and he was already one of the world's richest men. But he wanted more money—and more power. Xanatos glanced at his assistant, Owen Burnett. "It's time!" he told Owen. "Now we'll see if the legend about the Gargoyles is true."

The sun began to sink in the west. Xanatos scowled at the stone Gargoyles. They had not moved for a thousand years.

"Don't disappoint me," Xanatos said to them.

Suddenly, the ground began to rumble. Small cracks ripped across the Gargoyles' hard bodies. Lightning and thunder split the sky above. The Gargoyles burst out of their stone shells. They spread their wings. They were alive! The spell was broken!

"Yes!" Xanatos cried in triumph. "It has happened!"

Six Gargoyles stood before Xanatos. The first to come alive was a handsome gray-blue giant. Xanatos knew that this was their leader, Goliath.

The second to come alive had a wise face. He carried an ancient sword. This old one bent down and petted a Gargoyle that looked like a dog. It growled up at him happily.

Next were three younger Gargoyles. The brown one was small and mischievous looking. He leaped into the arms of the big-bellied blue Gargoyle beside him. The youngest was orange with wild hair. His eyes shone bright in his friendly face.

The Gargoyles hugged each other. "We're alive!" they cried.

The clouds parted. The Gargoyles peered down from the castle tower. The rooftops of the huge city were spread below them. "What is this? Where are we?" they wondered.

"Come with me," Xanatos said. "I will explain." He led the Gargoyles into his office. "You are the last of your kind. A thousand years have passed since the spell was cast upon you."

The Gargoyles gasped.

"I learned of you from the Magus's ancient book," Xanatos went on. "The castle was flown high above the clouds from Scotland to here, New York City. And the spell was broken!"

Goliath frowned. "Why have you done this?"

"To see if the legend was true," Xanatos replied. "I want to be your friend. We can do a lot for each other. And soon—"

Suddenly, there was a loud noise. It came from the sky. A helicopter was landing on the roof of the skyscraper.

"What's this?" Xanatos exclaimed. He ran onto the roof and cried out in surprise. Men with laser weapons jumped out of the helicopter.

"They are attacking the castle!" the old Gargoyle shouted.

Goliath leaped toward the army of men. "We must battle these humans!" he cried. "We must protect the castle!"

CHAPTER 2

The Gargoyles swooped down on the attackers!

"Look out! Monsters!" the attackers yelled. They fell back in fear.

"Secure the area!" their leader commanded. He aimed his weapon at David Xanatos.

The other attackers fired at the Gargoyles. The Gargoyles had never seen weapons like these before. But they managed to dodge the deadly laser blasts—all except the old Gargoyle. He dropped to his knees. He was hit in the chest.

The orange Gargoyle charged the attacker who had hit the old one. "Leave him alone!" the youngster shouted. The attacker answered by tossing a bomb right at him!

"Look out!" Goliath shouted.

The small brown Gargoyle jumped up. He caught the bomb. He took aim and threw it right back.

BLAM! Three of the attackers went flying!

"These must be evil sorcerers!" the old one cried.

"Maybe so," Goliath yelled back. "Still, we will protect the castle! It is all we have left!"

But as he spoke, another bomb

exploded. Goliath was blown off the rooftop!

"Arrngh!" Goliath cried as he tumbled down, down, down—heading straight for the pavement below. He quickly reached out and sank his claws deep into the stone blocks of the building. He stopped his fall.

Goliath climbed up the side of the wall. Bits of stone crumbled all around him. The walls had been loosened by the explosion. Goliath swung himself back onto the roof just as a huge block of stone fell to the street below.

Then the leader of the attackers appeared. He clutched a black briefcase. "Got it!" he shouted to his men. "Let's get out of here. We have what we came for!"

The attackers backed away, blasting their laser weapons to keep the Gargoyles from following them. Then they scrambled up ropes that led to the helicopter.

The helicopter lifted high into the night sky. In an instant, it disappeared.

"We fought them off, lads!" cried the impish brown Gargoyle.

"They ran like rabbits!" his big-bellied blue friend agreed. Even the watchdog barked in triumph.

"Thank you, my friends." Xanatos smiled warmly at the Gargoyles.

"Why were you attacked?" Goliath asked him.

"The richer you are, the more enemies you have," Xanatos replied. "Without your help, who knows what might have happened?"

Goliath narrowed his eyes. "Someone I once trusted said the same thing to me. Then he let my people be destroyed anyway."

"Goliath," Xanatos said, "I know

you've been treated badly by humans in the past. But you can trust me. I am your true friend."

Goliath frowned. "You broke the spell that imprisoned us, Xanatos," he said. "And for that we are grateful. But we will never trust humans again."

CHAPTER 3

A crowd gathered on the street below the Eyrie Building. They could see that something was happening on the roof. But what?

"Get back!" the police shouted, trying to hold back the curious onlookers.

A beautiful young woman pushed her way through the crowd. She had long dark hair and large brown eyes. She stepped toward the policeman and flipped open an ID card holder.

"Elisa Maza, NYPD. Detective Second Class," she announced. "What's going on?"

"Must be quite a party going on up there. Be careful, Detective," the policeman warned. "Watch out for falling rocks!"

Just then, a huge block of stone crashed at their feet. Elisa studied it carefully. "Odd," she muttered. "Claw marks."

What animal—what thing—was strong enough to dig deep claw marks into solid stone? Elisa glanced at the skyscraper towering overhead. She had no idea—but she was going to find out!

Elisa rode the elevator straight to the top of the Eyrie Building. Owen Burnett hurried to meet her.

"I heard shooting up here," Elisa said.

"I want an explanation—now."

"You'd better see Mr. Xanatos," Owen said. Elisa pushed past him into Xanatos's office. Xanatos rose from his desk. He smiled at Elisa.

"We just fought off an attack, Detective. Someone tried to steal my company's secrets. But it's over. Nothing for you to worry about."

Xanatos ordered Owen to take Elisa back to the elevator. The elevator doors opened, and she stepped inside. But as soon as Owen turned his back, Elisa jumped out. Then she sneaked back onto the roof of the building. Something was up there. Something to worry about—she was sure of it.

Elisa climbed to the top of the castle tower. Suddenly, she heard a low growling noise behind her. She spun around and drew out her weapon. "Okay, pal— let me see you!" she cried.

Red eyes glowed at her in the dark. And she was certain that she saw sharp fangs. Then a four-legged monster leaped at her!

Elisa jumped back—and slammed into another monster. She whirled. The monster's skin was blue-gray. It had sharp claws. Great wings sprang from its shoulders. A living Gargoyle!

It was Goliath. As he stepped toward Elisa, she stumbled backward—and tripped over the edge of the roof.

"Look out!" Goliath yelled.

But Elisa was already falling. Headfirst, she plunged toward the street. Goliath leaped off the roof and glided after her. He snatched Elisa in midair and landed her safely on a narrow ledge. Then he wrapped her arms around his neck and carried her back to the roof.

"What were you doing in my castle?" Goliath asked.

Elisa's jaw dropped. "You—you can talk? Who—who are you?"

"My kind have no names. But you humans call me Goliath."

"Your kind…you mean there are more of you?"

"Barely," Goliath growled. As he spoke, five dark shapes stepped out from the shadows. It was the other Gargoyles. They gathered to stare at Elisa. She gasped when she saw them.

"Now, what are you doing here?" Goliath asked again.

"I'm a detective," Elisa explained. "I find answers to hard questions. I have a question tonight—why were stone blocks falling off this building? What's going on?"

"It is a long, sad tale," Goliath said. Then he told her the whole story.

"So a thousand years ago," she said, "you were betrayed by the one human you trusted. Do any other humans here know about you?"

"Only Xanatos," Goliath replied.

"Good," Elisa said thoughtfully. "Because—"

Goliath looked toward the horizon. The sun was rising. "You have to go," Goliath quickly told Elisa. "Now."

"Wait!" she protested. "Will I see you again? You saved my life. I should do something for you. Let me show you the city. You need to know how it works—if you're going to survive here."

The old one frowned. "She is a human," he warned Goliath.

"Yet, if we are to defend the castle," Goliath said slowly, "we will need to know this place. Very well—Elisa. Let us meet tomorrow night." He stretched a mighty arm toward a distant building. "But not here. Over there, on that rooftop."

When Elisa had gone, the orange Gargoyle tugged on Goliath's wing. "Was that a new friend, Goliath?" he asked.

Goliath frowned. "That was—a detective," he answered.

Just then, Xanatos called Goliath into his office. "I need your help," Xanatos cried. "The attackers—they stole something very valuable. Three of these—"

He held up a computer disk. "Think of these as magic spell books. They are very powerful! You must get them back for me."

"Perhaps you should use a...detective," Goliath suggested.

"You are learning fast," Xanatos said in surprise. "But I can't go to the police. What if they found you here? They would probably want to lock you up. Remember—you are the only Gargoyles left in the world."

Goliath was thoughtful. "So what

exactly would you like us to do?"

"Those thieves were hired by my enemy—a powerful company called Cyberbiotics," Xanatos said. "They have taken the disks to three different places." Xanatos switched on a video monitor. Goliath watched in amazement as pictures flickered across the screen.

"The first disk is in a tower in the bay," Xanatos said. "The second is hidden deep beneath the city in a tunnel."

Xanatos pointed to a third picture. "The last disk is in a huge airship in the sky. You must attack all three places at once, so they can't warn each other."

"Surely humans are better suited to help you," Goliath said.

"You Gargoyles have special talents," Xanatos said urgently. "Humans are not as strong—or as loyal!"

"But this is not like protecting the castle," Goliath said. "It will endanger the lives of my friends. I cannot risk that."

"I understand." Xanatos wrapped an arm around Goliath's shoulders as he led him to the door. Hidden in his palm was a tiny object. Goliath felt nothing as Xanatos stuck the object to Goliath's back. "But remember," Xanatos continued, "our enemies are evil. They'll use the disks for evil—unless you stop them."

When Goliath had gone, Xanatos pressed a hidden button. A secret panel slid open in the wall. A strange figure waited in the shadows.

"Don't worry," Xanatos told the shadowy figure. "It won't be long now. Everything is going according to plan."

CHAPTER 4

Dawn came. The Gargoyles slept while the sun shone. At sunset, the walls of the castle began to shake. Stone skins cracked and shattered like eggshells. One by one, the Gargoyles spread their wings and greeted the night with roars of life.

"I am hungry!" said the big-bellied Gargoyle.

"You are always hungry." The little brown one chuckled.

"I want to explore this city!" the orange Gargoyle said.

"Can we go, Goliath?" the brown one begged. "Please?"

"Very well," Goliath told them. "But be careful. This new world is dangerous. Be sure you do not let the humans see you."

One by one, the youngsters glided off to explore their new world. Goliath spread his wings and glided off to meet Elisa.

Elisa waited on the nearby rooftop. "Goliath!" she exclaimed as he appeared. She hurried toward him. Just then, a dark form emerged from behind a corner. Elisa gasped.

"You—what are you doing here?" Goliath asked.

It was the old Gargoyle. "Making sure

Over one thousand years ago in Scotland, the Gargoyles guarded Castle Wyvern and all who lived there.

One terrible day, the castle was attacked. Most of the Gargoyles were shattered to bits.

Only six
Gargoyles
survived—and
each of them
was cast under
an evil spell that
turned them to
stone by day and
night.

But one thousand years later, the spell was
broken! And the Gargoyles awakened to find...

...their castle sitting on top of a large skyscraper in New York City!

David Xanatos, a rich businessman, was the one who broke the spell. "You can trust me," he tells the Gargoyles. "I am your friend."

Down on the street below the skyscraper, Detective Elisa Maza studies a huge block of stone. "Claw marks?" she wonders.

Elisa Maza meets the Gargoyles and promises to keep their castle a secret.

Meanwhile, Xanatos reveals a secret to the Gargoyles. Demona, Goliath's second-in-command, is also alive!

But Demona has changed over the years. She tells Goliath about her evil plan to rule the world!

Demona has someone on her side—Xanatos! And they won't let anyone get in their way—not even a Gargoyle.

"If you are not my friend, you are my enemy!"
Demona cries as she fires a deadly blast at
Goliath.

Elisa leaps at
Demona to
save Goliath!

As the sun rises, Goliath thanks Elisa for saving him—and for helping the Gargoyles defeat Demona and Xanatos.

you were not tricked, lad," he answered.

Elisa faced him bravely. "Why don't you come with us?" she asked. "You'll see I can be trusted. Okay, Mister..." Elisa paused. "What's your name, anyway? I don't know what to call you."

"Must you humans name everything?" the old one replied.

Elisa shrugged. "Things need names."

"Does the sky have a name?" he asked. "Does the river?"

"The river's called the Hudson," Elisa answered, smiling.

"Fine." The old one sighed. "Then I will be *Hudson* as well."

"Great," Elisa said. "Hudson it is!"

"Let's be off," Goliath said impatiently. "Coming, Hudson?"

"I think not," Hudson replied. "Now that I see you are all right, I will return to the castle." He spread his wings and glided away.

"Well," Elisa said to Goliath. "It's just the two of us. Let's go—there's so much to see!"

Goliath lifted Elisa in his arms and leaped from the rooftop. For hours they explored the huge city. Goliath was amazed by what he saw.

"Let's take a quiet walk through Central Park," Elisa suggested. "Trees and meadows won't seem so strange to you."

Goliath and Elisa strolled through the park. Suddenly, Goliath jerked up his head.

"Goliath, what is it?" Elisa asked.

"Argh!" Goliath cried out as something sharp stung him in the arm. Then he saw them. "The attackers from last night!" he shouted. "Quick, Elisa—you must run!"

But they were already surrounded. An attacker flung a rope around Goliath.

"Just tying up loose ends," he said. "Once you're out of the way, we'll go after the others like you."

"No!" Elisa leaped at the attacker, catching him by surprise. Goliath was able to throw off the rope.

Elisa grabbed Goliath's hand. They raced across the moonlit park. But Goliath was moving very slowly.

"In here!" Elisa pulled Goliath under a footbridge. Goliath shook his head as if to clear it. "What is...wrong with me...?"

Elisa plucked a dart from his arm. "This! They put a drug in you!" Then she pulled a small object off his back. "And this is how they found us. It's a radio transmitter! It sends a signal to tell them where you are!"

Goliath looked at it closely. "Some form of magic led them to us?"

"That's one way of putting it," Elisa said.

"But how did this…transmitter…get on me?" Goliath asked.

"Good question." Elisa stared at the transmitter. On its back was a picture of a beetle. "I've seen this somewhere," she murmured. "It's the symbol of a company. But which one?"

A stray dog wandered past. "Here, boy." Elisa attached the transmitter to the stray. The dog ran off. "Let them follow him for a while." Elisa smiled grimly. "Now, let's get out of here."

Goliath struggled to keep up with Elisa. He glanced up. The sky was brightening overhead. "Too late," he gasped. "I'll never make it back…before sunrise…"

"I don't get it," Elisa said. "What happens at sunrise?"

Goliath didn't have time to answer. Just then, the sun came out. The masked men appeared, coming closer.

"Goliath, we've got to move!" Elisa said urgently. But when she turned to him, she screamed.

CHAPTER 5

Goliath had turned to stone. He was a helpless statue!

Elisa stared at him. She couldn't believe it. The attackers were only a few yards away. Elisa leaped out of the bushes and ran. She crossed right in front of the masked attackers.

"There she goes!" The leader pointed after her.

"Wait—where's the Gargoyle?" another attacker asked.

"We'll track him later with the transmitter! First get her!"

Elisa ran faster than she ever had before. Her sides ached, but she kept moving. Then she spotted a wooden boat house through the trees. She ran inside, slamming the door behind her. "Safe!" Elisa gasped.

But she had spoken too soon. KAPOW! Laser blasts shattered the walls above her head. She had to get out of there. "Here goes nothing!" Elisa said.

She crawled toward the open end of the boat house. The boat house stood over the lake. Elisa jumped into the water and dove deep under the surface. BLAM! The boat house exploded behind her. It was totally destroyed. But Elisa was safe.

Elisa swam to a nearby dock. The

attackers were gone. Quickly she pulled herself out of the water and dashed back to Goliath's side. There she waited as the long day passed.

At sunset, the ground beneath them began to tremble.

"Goliath! Are you okay?" she asked as he stretched to life.

"Of course," he answered. "Sleep heals our wounds. But—did you stay here with me all day?"

"Yes…somebody had to make sure they didn't find you."

"You saved my life." He held out his hand.

Elisa put her small hand in his huge one. "Well, you saved mine when I fell off the roof," she replied. "So now we're even."

Goliath smiled. "Now I must return to the castle." He rose and spread his wings. "My friends will be worried."

"Meet me later tonight," Elisa called. "At the same rooftop!"

Back at the castle, Goliath greeted his friends. "Hudson, it is good to see you!" he cried.

"Hudson?" the others repeated.

The old one roared with laughter as Goliath explained his new name. The others quickly chose names for themselves. They picked names that they had seen when they explored the city.

"Call me *Brooklyn*," the wild-haired orange one said proudly.

"I will be *Lexington*," said the brown Gargoyle.

"Broadway!" the big-bellied blue one announced. "That's me! And you can be *Bronx*," he told the watchdog, who barked happily.

Hudson drew Goliath aside. "What happened to you, lad?" he asked. "Where were you all this day?"

"Hiding from our enemies," Goliath answered. Before he could explain, Xanatos called him into his office.

"There's someone here I want you to meet." Xanatos slid open the secret panel in the wall. "An old friend."

"You!" Goliath gasped. "Alive?"

A blue-skinned, red-haired female Gargoyle stepped forward.

"Yes, Goliath," she said. "Your second-in-command. I have dreamed of this moment!" She pointed to Xanatos. "And this man has brought us back together! He calls me *Demona*."

"But...you were shattered by the Vikings!" Goliath cried.

"No," she told him. "I feared for your safety, so I left Castle Wyvern to find you. But I was too late. The Magus had already turned you to stone. He also cast his spell upon me. I slept until Xanatos found me. He brought me here—so that

41

we could all be together!"

Goliath led her outside. The other Gargoyles were overjoyed to see their second-in-command again.

"It's a miracle!" Hudson exclaimed. The youngsters hugged her, and the watchdog licked her hands.

Demona faced them all. "Xanatos told me of the stolen disks. I think we should help him get them back. After all, he saved us."

"I agree," Goliath said.

Xanatos was delighted. He gathered the Gargoyles and explained the plan of attack. "Goliath, you and Demona will enter the airship. You three," he told the youngsters, "will hit the tower." He turned to Hudson. "You and the watchdog will enter the tunnel."

The Gargoyles were ready. They agreed to meet back at the Eyrie Building. Then they took off.

Goliath and Demona boarded the airship according to plan. They searched through its empty hallways.

"Here!" Demona cried. "The computer laboratory!"

They crashed inside. The defenders of the airship were completely stunned. "Monsters!" they yelled. They stood frozen in surprise as Goliath and Demona wrestled their weapons away. In no time, the men lay helpless on the ground. It was over without a fight.

Goliath located the ship's computer and grabbed the stolen disk. "We have it," he told Demona. "Let's go!"

"No," Demona exclaimed. "We are not through yet."

She plunged her hand into the heart of the computer and pulled out a live wire. She used it to touch off a fire. Flames spread through the laboratory.

"What are you doing?" Goliath gasped

in horror. "Fire is deadly here! The airship will crash!"

"Fine. Then they will not be able to stop us." Demona kicked open a door. "Come on!"

"No! We cannot leave the humans to die!" Goliath protested.

"Do not worry. No one will know it was us." Demona shoved Goliath through the open door into midair. He caught an air current and glided away with Demona by his side. Seconds later, the helpless ship dove through the air. It plunged into the river.

From the shoreline, Elisa was watching. She saw the airship burst into flames. She saw it plummet into the river. And she saw two strange forms glide away. Elisa's eyes opened wide in disbelief. She recognized one of the forms. Goliath!

CHAPTER 6

Goliath and Demona returned to the Eyrie Building. The other Gargoyles waited on the roof. All three teams had been able to get the disks. The Gargoyles handed the disks over to Xanatos.

"My friends," he told them, "you have my deepest thanks. The knowledge on these disks will be put to good use—for humans and Gargoyles alike." Xanatos strode back into his office.

Goliath turned to Demona. "I have promised to meet a human friend," he told her. "I will be back soon."

"Aside from Xanatos, we have no human friends!" Demona protested. "Goliath, you should know that!"

"I cannot make war upon an entire world," he told her.

"The humans must pay for what they did to us!" she cried.

"You have changed, Demona. You have become hard, unforgiving." Goliath's eyes flashed. "You are not as I remember you. I am going to see my friend now."

Demona growled deep in her throat as she watched him take off. "So be it," she said.

Xanatos watched the scene on the video monitor in his office. "Goliath is too hard to control," he remarked to Owen. "A pity. We shall have to destroy him."

Meanwhile, on the nearby rooftop, Elisa was waiting. "Where have you been?" she asked Goliath. "I've been looking all over town for you! There have been three robberies by some kind of *creatures*. And I saw you and another Gargoyle flying away from the airship wreck. What's this all about?"

"Three disks were stolen from Xanatos," Goliath explained. "We returned them to him."

Elisa took a piece of paper from her pocket and showed it to him. It was a sketch of the beetle. "Remember this?" she asked. "It's the picture on the transmitter. This is the symbol of a company, all right. A company that's owned by David Xanatos!"

Goliath frowned in confusion. "Are you saying that Xanatos attacked us in the park?"

"That's exactly what I'm saying. He probably put that transmitter on you himself!" Elisa told him.

"But those were the same men who stole the disks from him!"

"Goliath, nothing was stolen from Xanatos. I'm a detective, remember? I checked." Elisa paused for a deep breath.

"Xanatos pretended he was attacked. He did it to make you think his enemies stole those disks from him. But the disks you took belonged to Xanatos's enemy. Xanatos tricked you! He used you! He's been using you from the beginning!"

Goliath's eyes glowed with anger.

Elisa stepped close to the Gargoyle. "Listen, Goliath. We haven't known each other very long. You have no reason to trust humans. But you've got to trust somebody in this world. And I think you'd be better off trusting me—than Xanatos."

Goliath crumpled the paper in his hand. He frowned. Then he spread his wings—and leaped from the rooftop with a mighty roar that shattered the night.

CHAPTER 7

Xanatos paced across his office. Owen and Demona waited patiently. Beside them stood five bulky objects that were hidden under a huge sheet.

"We don't need the Gargoyles anymore," Xanatos announced. "Now I have the disks. And with them, I have created these. The Gargoyles' replacements!"

Xanatos whipped off the sheet.

Underneath it were five enormous robots—shaped like Gargoyles. Their wings were made of razor-sharp steel. Their arms were powerful laser weapons.

"These robots are better than Gargoyles," Xanatos exclaimed. "They are steel, not stone. They don't sleep during the day. They fly instead of glide. And best of all, they will always obey me!"

Xanatos ordered the robots to stand on the roof until Goliath returned to the castle.

When Goliath returned he stared at the robots in shock.

"Xanatos!" Goliath gasped. "What are these things?"

Xanatos did not answer. "Attack!" he ordered the robots.

The robots unfolded their sharp metal wings. They aimed their laser weapons at the Gargoyles. SWOOSH!

"Look out!" Hudson shouted. The lasers hit the stone wall. Chunks of stone flew into the air. The Gargoyles leaped away, but Broadway and Lexington were hit. They fell to the ground, stunned. Brooklyn and Bronx rushed to their sides. Together they dragged Broadway and Lexington to safety behind a rock wall.

Goliath roared in anger. He slammed one robot into the castle wall. KRAACK! It blew up!

Goliath grabbed a second robot and aimed it straight toward a third. KABAAM! The two robots slammed into each other. They broke into jagged pieces. Scraps of metal showered onto the roof.

Hudson drew his sword. The fourth robot raised its lasers and aimed at the old Gargoyle. But before it could fire,

Hudson lashed out with his mighty blade. The sword slashed through metal as if it were butter. He had sliced the robot in two!

Xanatos watched. He was not happy. "My *Steel Clan* isn't performing as well as I'd hoped," he said.

"There is only one robot left!" Demona warned. "We must do something!"

"We will," Xanatos assured her with a sinister smile. "I haven't given up yet. Come!" Xanatos quickly led Demona into his office.

On the roof, the last robot hurled itself straight toward Brooklyn and Bronx. They had their backs turned because they were helping Lexington and Broadway. The two Gargoyles didn't see the robot coming.

But Goliath and Hudson saw—and they were ready. From their hiding place in the tower above, they watched. Just at the right moment, the two strong Gargoyles threw their weight against the tower's ancient wall. At the same instant, the robot passed below them. The tower wall toppled. Huge stones crashed down toward the roof. The robot raised its lasers—too late. The huge stones crushed the robot's metal body. There was an explosion—and then silence.

Lexington jumped to his feet. "We did it," he exclaimed. "It is over! And we won!"

"Did you?" a voice asked.

The Gargoyles turned.

"Demona!" Goliath cried out in disbelief.

The female Gargoyle stood on the pile of fallen stones. In her hands, she held a deadly weapon. Next to her stood Xanatos, pointing a laser gun.

Demona smiled an evil smile. "Your young friend spoke too soon, Goliath," she said calmly. "It is not over yet!"

CHAPTER 8

"You are a fool!" Demona told Goliath. "This is all your fault! If only you'd taken the rest of us away from the castle that night! The plan was perfect. It would have succeeded!"

"The plan?" Goliath was stunned. "You knew of the captain's plan?"

"It was *my* plan, too!" Demona's eyes glinted with pride. "I made a bargain with the captain of the guards! I was to lead the Gargoyles out of the castle, leaving the Vikings to attack the humans!"

"Those humans let us live in peace," Goliath thundered.

"They called us monsters!" Demona cried out. "They deserved to die. With the humans gone, the castle would have been ours! But you ruined it!"

Goliath couldn't believe what he was hearing.

Demona stared at him coldly. "I knew the captain couldn't protect us from the Vikings. I fled! And I've stayed alive— because I don't trust anyone!"

"But why?" Goliath moaned. "Why did you do it?"

"You ask me that-—after how they treated us? They had to pay! All humans must pay for what they did to us!"

"There is good and evil in everyone!"

Goliath shouted back. "Human and Gargoyle alike! You should know that more than anyone. Don't you see, Demona?" Goliath paused. "None of this would have happened—if it weren't for *you*!"

"This is your last chance," Demona growled. "If you are not my friend, you are my enemy!" Demona aimed her weapon at his chest. "Good-bye, Goliath."

Suddenly, from out of the shadows, a figure leaped at Demona. It was Elisa! She hurled herself at Demona, and the evil Gargoyle was thrown off balance. Her weapon fired—and missed!

The blast slammed into the tower above them. Xanatos was standing underneath. He was hit by falling stones. He crumpled to the ground.

The blast shattered the tower. The thick stone building began to crumble—

with Demona and Elisa clinging to its huge blocks of stone.

"Eeeiaaah!" Elisa screamed as she was thrown into midair. Around her the heavy stones hurtled toward the street, thousands of feet below.

Goliath sprang into action. He dove down and saved Elisa. He returned her to the safety of the castle.

Goliath's keen eyes scanned the street below. The female Gargoyle had been thrown through the air, too. Where was she? Goliath wondered. Had she died in the fall?

"Demona!" he roared in fury and grief.

Then Goliath grabbed Xanatos. He lifted him over the edge of the building. Xanatos dangled in midair. The Gargoyle was about to throw him over the edge.

"No, Goliath!" Elisa shouted. "Don't! Don't do it! If you kill him, you'll be the same as evil Demona!"

"She's right, lad," Hudson yelled. "Is that what you want?"

Goliath paused. "No," he said quietly. Sighing, he let Xanatos go. Their battle was over.

Later, as dawn began to break, Xanatos was taken away to prison. Goliath and Elisa stood on the castle roof, gazing out over the city.

"It's nice to know I have at least one human friend," he said.

"I hope you have more," Elisa replied. "Lots more. But whether you do or not—I'll always be your friend, Goliath." Smiling, she added, "Same time tomorrow night?"

Goliath smiled back. "I wouldn't miss it."

The sun rose, and slowly he turned to stone again.

Elisa gazed over the sleeping city. There was good in it, and there was evil. She glanced at her new friend. And now there would be justice, too.